Kate Mosse

The Black Mountain

PAN BOOKS

First published 2022 by Pan Books
an imprint of Pan Macmillan
The Smithson, 6 Briset Street, London EC1M 5NR
EU representative: Macmillan Publishers Ireland Ltd, 1st Floor,
The Liffey Trust Centre, 117–126 Sheriff Street Upper,
Dublin 1, D01 YC43
Associated companies throughout the world
www.panmacmillan.com

ISBN 978-1-5290-8846-5

3 5 7 9 8 6 4 2

A CIP catalogue record for this book is available from the British Library.

Typeset by Palimpsest Book Production Ltd, Falkirk, Stirlingshire
Printed and bound by CPI Group (UK) Ltd, Croydon, CR0 4YY

Visit **www.panmacmillan.com** to read more about all our books
and to buy them. You will also find features, author interviews and
news of any author events, and you can sign up for e-newsletters
so that you're always first to hear about our new releases.

To my beloved Greg and Martha and Felix

Monday, 3 May 1706

Two days before

Chapter One

Ana looked down into the open grave. She felt anger burning in her chest, as red and hot as fire, but she would not cry. She dug her fingers into the palms of her hands until her rage passed. The pain cleared her mind.

It was a plain coffin, made from wood from the trees that covered the lower slopes of the mountain. This northern part of the island of Tenerife, where they lived in the shadow of the Black Mountain, was filled with pine forests and cedar groves. It was a green world, filled with vineyards. The south of Tenerife, or so Ana had heard, was dry and bare. Few trees grew there and it almost never rained. One day, she would go and see for herself.

It was a cool afternoon in early May. The sky was overcast, just right for a funeral – except, of course, there had been no service. A man who took his own life could not be buried in sacred ground. 'It is a mortal sin,' the priest had told her. The priest was a weasel-faced man, with bad breath and long, greasy hair. All the girls of the town knew to stay away from him.

Instead, Ana, her mother and brothers had come here – to this corner of their narrow strip of land – to bury their father beneath the vines. Just the family and one or two farmers who, like them, made a living from growing grapes and making wine.

Ana shivered, suddenly cold. She had been standing still for too long. She looked over her shoulder. Everyone else had gone, even her mother with her face hidden behind a black lace veil. Ana had felt someone touch her shoulder as they left. She didn't know whether it was in support or pity. Only the man who had been paid to dig the unmarked grave was still here. Leaning on his spade a few steps away, he was waiting for her to go so he could finish the job.

Ana looked down again. Someone had carved her father's name on the box – Tomas Perez. Nothing else. It wasn't much to show for a life.

'I'm sorry,' she whispered in Spanish. Ana made the sign of the cross, then dropped her offering – white and purple wild flowers – onto the lid of the coffin. There was a dull thud and the ribbon came undone, leaving the flowers scattered.

'Rest in peace, Papa,' she said, then she nodded to the labourer.

As Ana walked away, her long skirt sweeping the dust, she heard the sound of earth falling on the coffin, burying her father's earthly remains in the land he had loved so much.

Chapter Two

Ana walked down through the rows of vines, with their long, twisted roots, to the path that led to their house. Her head was full of troubled thoughts.

Her father had been found in a clearing, higher up the mountain. His leather bag and his eye glass were by his side. His shotgun was between his knees. It seemed he had pulled the trigger with a string and killed himself.

Ana could not accept that. She knew they owed money. But she didn't believe her father would have abandoned his wife and his sons. Her twin brothers were only eleven. They were good boys, though lazy. They needed their father. Most of all, Ana did not believe he would have left her to provide for the family on her own. The sole reason they were still growing grapes on their small patch of land was because she had worked so hard at his side.

'Papa . . .' she murmured, grief sticking in her throat.

She swallowed hard. When they had been told the news of her father's death a week ago, her mother had collapsed. It had fallen to Ana to identify his body and collect his things. She saw the blood on his hands and chest. She saw the red mark on his right index finger where he'd tied the string tight. But when she saw the empty socket where his right eye had been, Ana had been sick on the floor of the town hall.

The thought of that made her burn with shame. The mayor had not been kind. He was the brother of the town priest and a firm Catholic. He made it very clear how he judged her father for taking the coward's way out.

Ana suddenly felt dizzy. She had eaten nothing all day, save for a piece of dry bread and a small glass of sweet wine. Maybe that was why the world was spinning. Also, it was very humid. The air was still and heavy. Perhaps a storm was coming, though storms were rare at this time of the year.

Ana took off her straw hat. Like all the island women, she wore her hair parted in the middle and tied in a bun at the nape of her neck. She shook her long straight black hair loose. Before she had been cold, now she was too hot. When she wiped her damp hands with the corner of her petticoat, she saw the red ribbon around the hem had come loose. She sighed, realising she would have to mend it later. Another task to add to her growing list.

Ana was halfway home, but she was tired. She sat on a rock and looked north, down over the valley towards the town. Despite the greyness of the afternoon, there was colour all around. Usually, May was Ana's favourite time of year. She loved seeing the first rows of purple and green grapes on the vine. She loved all the wild flowers that grew on the slopes of the Black Mountain – yellow broom, pink and white wallflowers. The tall, red plants that sparkled like rubies. She loved the dragon trees and the palm trees swaying in the breeze, the pine trees and cedar trees.

Today, everything looked different.

She let her eyes focus on the Atlantic Ocean. From this high up, the view was so wide that she could see how the horizon wasn't straight but a curve. Higher in the middle and lower at the edges. The sea was wild in winter, the waves crashing on the rocks. Today the water was calm.

Her home town was the most important port in Tenerife, welcoming trading ships from all corners of the globe. They arrived with sugar and dyes for cloth and carried away the famous wine.

Wine from the Canary Islands was sent all over the world. It was an important port and a rich one.

At this time of day, Ana knew the fishermen would be mending their nets. Their wives would be smoking seaweed and gutting fish. The port was where her twin brothers – Pablo and Carlos – were often to be found watching the tall ships. They dreamt of a life on the sea, not a life tilling the soil. They talked of rigging and sails, of countries on the far side of the world.

From here, Ana could see all the white buildings of the town and the tall, thin spire of the church of Saint Ana. Her parents had named her after the saint – the patron saint of mothers – in gratitude at finally having a child who lived. Four babies before Ana had been born dead or lived only for a few hours. Two others died after her, then the twins came along. She thought of them often, those dead sisters and brothers she would never know.

So many ghosts.

Ana fanned herself with her hat, though it made no difference. There was an odd atmosphere this afternoon, as if something was about to happen, and a strange smell. She sniffed. It was like bad eggs.

Her thoughts, her emotions, were confused. She had waited until the burial, but now there was no excuse. She had to decide what – if anything – she was going to do. Standing by her father's grave, she had felt she could take on the world and win. Now she wasn't certain.

If only she was sure.

Her hand went to the pocket of her striped woollen skirt. Inside was the letter that her father had left behind on his final morning. Propped in the middle of the mantel above the fire, where it could not be missed. Ana took the letter out of her pocket. She had read it so many times, she knew it by heart.

This time, she saw something new. The clue she had been looking for.

She took a deep breath, then read the words one last time. She gave a grim smile. She knew it. She had been right all along. Hidden in plain sight, was a message from her father. A name. She picked out the six letters with her finger.

Ana breathed out.

To the men who controlled the town – with their rich clothes, fine-haired wigs and silver-tipped canes – this letter was further evidence that her father had meant to kill himself. That his death had not been a hunting accident. They were from Spain, not islanders, sent here to control trade. They ruled that her father had taken the coward's way out.

Ana didn't think her father's death was an accident either.

It was murder.

Chapter Three

Ana's eyes filled with tears.

Her dear father was dead, his body lying in the cold ground. Up till now, Ana had not allowed herself to weep. Now that she knew he had not left them willingly, somehow it meant she could allow herself to cry.

Ana shook her head. No, not yet. She had to stay strong.

She wiped her eyes with the back of her hand, then stood up. She felt scared but, mostly, she felt angry. If she was right about the message her father had left, then she had to be careful. His enemies were powerful men. If they knew Ana had worked out what they had done, they would silence her. The stakes were high. And she'd be putting her mother's and brothers' lives at risk, too.

From the way the shadows were falling on the mountainside, Ana knew the afternoon was almost done. She knew she should go home to their white house at the bottom of the slope with its brown wooden shutters and porch. Her mother would be worrying and she was Ana's responsibility now. But there was somewhere Ana had to go first. It wasn't far.

Holding her hat in her hand, she headed back up the slopes of the Black Mountain. Formed from volcanic rock thousands of years ago, the soil was good for growing grapes. It gave their wine its strong and special taste.

In the far distance, a long way south, she could see the white summit of the largest volcano that sat at the heart of Tenerife. Ana had never been that far south. Even in May, there was still snow on its peak. Sailors said that, at sunrise and at sunset when the sun was low, the volcano cast a shadow on the other islands many miles away across the sea.

The people who lived on the island before the Spanish came said that a devil lived inside. When the devil was angry, he sent fire and rock up into the sky.

Her father had told them the legend when they were little. And it was not just about the biggest volcano, but their Black Mountain too. The twins – Pablo and Carlos – had covered their ears, pretending to be scared, but Ana had loved the story and begged him to tell it again and again.

Night after night when she was little, Ana sat on the wooden balcony at the back of their house and watched the Black Mountain. She almost wished the devil would thunder and the sky would fill with fire. Year after year she waited, until she realised it was just a made-up story so that children did not go too close to the crater. Sometimes the earth trembled and shook – and there were tales of eruptions of fire and rock in other parts of the island – but the sky above their Black Mountain never did turn red.

Ana kept climbing. There was a slight breeze now. She could hear it whispering in the high grasses that grew on the upper slopes. A wall of yellow and cream reeds swaying in the afternoon air.

Her legs were tired, but she did not stop. Ana was sixteen and tall for a woman. She was broad, with strong shoulders. She took after her father and was proud of that. She loved her mother, but grief and tragedy had made Maria Perez fragile. She should never have been a farmer's wife. She had never recovered from the death of so many children. She was often ill and spent more time in church, praying to the saints, than outside with the sun on her face. Ana was built for working in the fields.

Ana arrived at the place. A narrow track was half hidden between two large broom trees, their yellow flowers like a burst of sunlight. It led to the clearing where her father had died. Ana had come here just after it had happened. There had been nothing to see. At least, nothing that told a different story – a man dead by his own hand, a splatter of rust-brown blood on the rocks and the ground, the marks of his boots in the dust.

A sense of sadness and of loss.

But for a week now, something had been preying on Ana's mind. Now that she had read her father's letter with fresh eyes, she hoped she might see something here she had missed before. Ana hoped that, if she listened hard enough, maybe his ghost might speak to her.

Chapter Four

Pablo and Carlos were bored. Their sister Ana had told them to stay at home. But as soon as they were sure their mother was asleep, they sneaked out of the house and went down to the port. She thought they spent too much time watching the tall ships, but she didn't understand. All they wanted was to go to sea.

The twins, as alike as peas in a pod, were sitting on the low wall by the beach. Banging their heels against the wall, they were seeing which of them could throw stones the furthest.

The boys took after their mother. They were small and pale, with long brown curly hair to their shoulders. Everyone struggled to tell them apart. But Pablo had a tiny scar on the inside of his left wrist. When he was six years old, he had torn his skin on a jagged piece of wire when trying to steal apples from an orchard. The older twin by five minutes, he had always been the more adventurous. Pablo was the leader, Carlos followed him.

'Haven't you more sense than to be throwing stones?'

The twins scrambled up from the wall just as the face of widow Silva loomed up from the black sand below them.

'You're old enough to know better,' she said. 'Haven't you something useful to do?'

Carlos pulled a face. 'Not today.'

Pablo jabbed him in the ribs with his elbow. Carlos remembered they weren't to tell anyone about the burial.

'How old are you?' Carlos blurted out.

Carlos had always been scared of widow Silva. She was tall and broad. Dressed from head to toe in black, with a small white collar, her grey hair was parted in the middle and tied into a bun. A comb held her widow's veil in place over her head and shoulders. Her face was turned brown by the sun and criss-crossed by a thousand lines.

'You should be ashamed of yourself, asking such a question,' she said.

Carlos flushed. 'Everyone's got to be something.'

'People don't like being asked their age.'

Pablo shielded his eyes and stared at her. 'Why not?'

Widow Silva leaned towards the boy, casting a shadow across his face.

'Because it makes them think about dying,' she said quietly. 'No one likes to do that.'

Although the boys were young and healthy, they both shivered.

'Come on,' Pablo said quickly. Pulling his twin down from the wall, they ran across the black sand towards the harbour.

Widow Silva watched them go, wondering why the Perez boys were so jumpy.

She looked around, but there was no sign of their mother. That wasn't unexpected. She was a timid creature. Maria Perez rarely came out of the house except to go to church. She went to confess her sins on Fridays and to Mass on Sundays. She never came down to the port.

Even before the family's recent troubles, Mrs Perez had seemed scared of her own shadow. Since the attack on their vineyards last January, she'd withdrawn even further. The death of her husband, Tomas, must have been the final straw and everyone knew there were money troubles.

Widow Silva shook her head. She knew what it was to lose a husband – hers had been lost at sea – but life carried on. A woman had no choice but to carry on.

She was feeling every one of her sixty years in her bones today. Nothing was easy. She pulled her veil over her shoulders and walked slowly over the black sand towards the local fishing boats. She wondered where Ana was. Ana usually kept a close eye on her brothers, trying to keep them out of trouble. The old woman sucked her teeth. Ana had her hands full with those boys.

A few moments later, widow Silva arrived at her smoking racks. She put down her basket, filled with dried seaweed, and sat heavily on her stool. Taking out her tinder box, she struck a piece of flint against the back of the blade of her knife. The sparks jumped away from the flint and settled in the dry tinder. She leant over and blew. The tinder was in a small circle of black stones. It began to glow and then the glow became a flame.

'Pass me that dry seaweed,' she said.

The thin boy in torn clothes, hiding behind the fishing boat, jumped. 'How did you know I was here?'

She grunted. 'You're always here when I light the fire.'

Rudi grabbed a handful of seaweed. 'Is this enough?'

'For now.'

Careful not to stare at him, she put the seaweed on top of the burning tinder. It started to burn, giving off a beautiful smell of salt and earth. She passed Rudi the delicate wooden struts of the smoking rack.

'Hold this.'

The boy stepped back as if he'd been struck. 'I can't.'

'You can,' she said firmly, and looked the other way as he struggled to balance the wooden pieces on his withered arm. Rudi had been born too early, and his left arm and left foot were as twisted as the roots of a vine. He could not climb or run like other boys, but he was clever, as sharp as a tack.

'Thank you,' she said, taking the last strut from his hand and putting it in place.

She reached down into an old pot, full of briny water. She took out a dozen small, silver-backed fish with blank dead eyes, and laid them on the smoking rack one by one.

Rudi edged closer.

'Once they've dried, how long will they last?' he asked.

'Long enough to be put aside in case the fishing boats can't go out.'

'Is a storm coming?'

Widow Silva looked at the horizon through the gap in the high harbour wall that protected the port. The Atlantic Ocean was flat and dark. But even here, right down by the water, the air was humid and heavy. There was something unsettling in the stillness.

'I don't think so . . .' She turned and looked inland towards the Black Mountain. 'But something's coming.'

Rudi followed her gaze. The lower slopes were all green with grass. Higher up the land was dry and brown. Over the mountain, the sky was white. Everything looked the same to him.

'What do you mean?' he asked.

The old woman shook her head. 'I don't know. I am old, so perhaps I imagine what is not there . . .' Pressing her hands on her knees, she hoisted herself to her feet. 'Stay here and look after the fish for me.'

'Where are you going?'

Widow Silva did not seem to hear. 'Keep them in the way of the smoke, but out of the flames.'

'Where are you going?' he asked again.

'Don't let the fire go out.'

*

At first, Rudi enjoyed his task.

It was fun to pile the seaweed onto the flames and see the fish change colour as they dried. But then he put too much seaweed on the fire in one go and the flames leapt up, scorching the tail-fins of the fish. He hobbled to the rock pools and found some wet weed to damp down the flames. It seemed to work, until he realised the smell was different. The dry weed smelt of salt and good earth. The wet weed smelt of things that were rotten.

Rudi bit his lip to stop himself from crying. Whatever he did, he failed. The other boys made fun of him. They all told him he was useless. Pablo was the worst. Yet again, he had proved them right. He couldn't even keep a fire going.

He wished the earth would open and swallow him up.

Chapter Five

In the clearing on the Black Mountain, Ana was looking down at the patch of earth where her father had died.

Ana loved the sound of birdsong. She loved to watch the tiny blue birds dart in and out of the trees, or to see a flock of wild canaries. But, today, it was completely quiet. Not even a kestrel flying high in the sky broke the silence. Perhaps, she wondered, the birds knew what had happened here and were showing their respect.

At that moment, a glint of sun came out from behind the clouds and turned the ground golden. Ana allowed herself to smile. Nature cared nothing for the lives of women or of men.

The sky was now an expanse of white with the glow of the sun behind it. There was a strange kind of a haze. From this high up, it was easy to imagine all the other islands surrounding Tenerife. Her father always called them 'seven stars on a blue sky'.

With a stab of memory, she remembered her

father's words the night of the attack on their vines. Four men, their faces covered in black hoods, had stolen onto their land with fire in their hands. If their friend Antonio had not been there, they would have lost everything.

After the danger was over, Antonio had taken her mother and brothers back to the house. Ana had stayed in the vineyard with her father to keep watch in case the attackers came back.

It had been a cold night in January and her father had wrapped his pale brown blanket around her to keep her warm. All the working men of the island wore this same long woollen shawl with a striped blue pattern around the edges.

As they'd sat in the darkness, her father had pointed to the night sky and told her it was a very special night. Ana had been angry. She didn't understand how he could be so calm after what had just happened. They had nearly lost everything.

'Ask me why,' he'd said.

When she hadn't answered, he had laughed.

'Well, I'll tell you all the same. Because the sky is so clear tonight, you can see the maidens. Look.'

Despite herself, Ana tilted her head back and stared.

'How many stars can you see?' he asked.

'Seven,' she said.

He nodded. 'The seven maidens in the sky, like the seven islands. This is our life, Ana. Here on the Lucky Islands. And Tenerife is the luckiest island of them all.'

Ana balled her hands into fists. 'After what's just happened, Papa, how can you think we are lucky? Why aren't you angry? Why aren't you—'

He rested his hand gently on her arm.

'Life is hard for most people, Ana,' he said. 'We are as lucky as we deserve to be. We are alive. We still have our vines. They did not win.'

Standing in the clearing now, remembering her dear father's voice, she felt tears come to her eyes again.

Suddenly, Ana felt the ground shake and her legs went from under her. The next thing she knew, she was sprawled in the dirt with her breath knocked out of her.

Sometimes the earth complained. Every island child knew this, the adults talked of this. There were sometimes tremors on the mountain, though nothing ever changed. But she had never felt anything so strong before.

Ana pressed both hands flat on the ground. No movement, no sound, nothing. She listened, waited, expecting another shift. Another lurch, a shaking of the earth. But nothing more happened. Everything was calm, everything was still.

But now she was aware of butterflies in her stomach. She realised she had fallen in the exact place her father had been found. Ana tried not to think about her father's head snapped back by the force of the bullet. Or his long black hair matted with blood. It was a sight she would never forget for as long as she lived. Instead, she forced herself to look at the red stain on the rock, now turned rust-brown by the fierce Tenerife sun.

She sat back against the rough surface of the boulder. She closed her eyes, trying to imagine his final moments. Had there been one murderer or more? Was her father aware he was in danger? Were his last moments full of fear or full of love for his family?

If he had shot himself, how had he done it? The muzzle of his shotgun was long. It would be very difficult to fire. She was about as tall as her father. Ana drew up her knees and pictured him wedging the gun between his boots. She pictured the deep mark on his finger where the twine had marked his skin. She mimed how he might have tied the string around the trigger, winding it round the butt of the gun so it pulled away from him.

Her eyes shot open. Of course! That was it.

Standing in the town hall, looking down at the dead body of her father, she'd seen the mistake his murderers had made. At the time, she had not understood. The red mark where the string had cut into his skin was on his right forefinger, but that was wrong.

Her father was left-handed in everything except for writing. In lessons, when he was a boy, the priest had tied his left hand behind his back to force him to use his right hand. He was beaten when he made a mistake. The hard lesson had worked. Her father signed documents with his right hand. When he had reported the attack on the vines at the town hall, he had used his right hand to write his name – Tomas Perez. But he used his left hand for everything else – chopping wood, tending the vines, for shooting.

Her father would never have fired his shotgun with his right hand, but the men who'd killed him hadn't known that. They had tied the string onto the wrong finger.

Chapter Six

Ana scrambled to her feet.

She had been away from home for too long, but she had to speak to her father's closest friend, Antonio. He lived further up the mountain. He would advise her what she should do.

Antonio was a hermit, choosing to spend his days alone in a shack on the slopes of the Black Mountain. He kept a nanny goat for milk and hardly ever came down into the town. His clothes were different from most islanders'. He wore breeches and a doublet. His hair and beard were grey, but no one knew how old he was.

Rumours surrounded him like an autumn mist. Some said he was mad, others that he was a wealthy landowner who had lost a fortune. Some said he was an outsider from another of the Canary Islands or, even, from the mainland. Others claimed he had been shipwrecked on the north coast of Tenerife and was in hiding. They said he was a pirate, that he was a sailor, that he was a spy for the king of Spain. Antonio denied nothing, said nothing, just continued with his quiet business.

All Ana knew was that Antonio was her father's most trusted friend. Like her father, he stood firm against the few rich men who controlled the town. The mayor and the priest were brothers and part of a wealthy wine-making family from Spain. A third brother lived on the mainland and bought and sold wine. The only sister was married to a man with a fleet of ships and plenty of money. None of them had any respect for island ways.

When the mayor had tried to force her father to sell their land to him, it was Antonio who had helped the Perez family stand against them. And when men came in the night with burning torches to destroy their vines, it had been Antonio who raised the alarm.

Ana ran back along the path and was about to start the climb to Antonio's shack, when a voice stopped her in her tracks.

'Ana!'

Her name echoed across the mountainside.

'Ana!'

She turned. On the slope behind her, she could see one of the twins waving his arms. She thought it was Pablo. Though the twins were the same to look at, their characters were quite different. Pablo was loud, always shouting. Carlos was quiet, always listening.

Ana mimed to show she couldn't hear.

'You have to come! Mama wants you.'

She still couldn't make out what he was saying, but from his hand signals she realised what he wanted. She was needed at home. Her visit to Antonio would have to wait until tomorrow.

With a sigh, Ana turned and walked down to join her brother.

Tuesday, 4 May 1706

The day before

Chapter Seven

The following morning, Ana was awake before daylight. She had hardly slept.

It had been a long evening. Her mother had been very upset when Ana got back – it seemed visitors had come to the house – so Ana didn't mention where she'd been, nor how she'd felt the ground shake.

By the time Ana had made a simple supper of cheese and bread – and persuaded her mother to drink a little wine to help her sleep – it was dark. Pablo and Carlos were restless. They argued over their father's eye glass until Ana took it away from both of them. To calm them down, she read aloud from the Bible – their favourite story was Jonah and the Whale – until the oil lamp burnt low.

When, at last, the twins were in bed, Ana found she could not sleep. Her head was spinning with everything that had happened during the day. As she lay there, waiting for the dawn, she could hear the rumbling of the Black Mountain in the distance.

*

'I will be back as soon as I can,' Ana said, hooking her father's leather bag over her shoulder. 'Leave Mama to rest. If anyone comes, don't let them in.'

'But there's nothing to do inside,' Carlos said.

Ana gave a short laugh. 'The table needs polishing, the tiles need washing, the—'

'That's girls' work,' Pablo said.

Ana turned on him. 'What did you say?'

Pablo turned red. Carlos, always the more timid of the two of them, looked at his boots.

'Other boys don't have to do housework,' Pablo said.

'Other boys work in the fields,' she said sharply. 'Would you prefer that?'

Pablo shrugged. 'I wouldn't mind.'

Ana knew he was not telling the truth. Their father had wanted his sons to fall in love with making wine, in the same way that she had. Ana enjoyed every part of the process – the pruning of the vines, watching the first grapes come, the harvesting and the long, long days and nights of turning grapes into wine. She loved writing the labels to be placed on each oak cask. But her brothers showed no interest at all.

'Very well,' she said. 'I will speak to our foreman and arrange for you to start tomorrow.'

Behind her back, she felt the twins exchange wild glances.

'Of course,' she added, 'it will mean no more visiting the port in the afternoons. You will have no time. But if that's what you wish . . .'

Ana took her shawl from the hook on the back of the door and started to leave.

'Wait!' Pablo called.

Ana kept her face stern. 'What is it?'

'I was . . .' He pulled a face. 'When we have finished in the kitchen, what should we do next?'

Ana smiled. 'After all the chores are done, you may go down to the port and buy fish for our supper. Go to widow Silva. Her fish is always fresh.'

Carlos threw his arms around her waist.

'Thank you!'

Ana kissed the top of Carlos's head and put her hand on Pablo's shoulder.

'So long as you both remember there are no boys' tasks and girls' tasks in this house any more, just things that need to be done. Do you understand?'

The twins nodded.

Ana smiled. 'Now, will you pass me my hat?'

Carlos looked at the hook. 'It's not there.'

She frowned. 'It must be. I always put it there.'

'See for yourself,' Pablo said.

Ana realised she must have left it in the clearing yesterday afternoon. No matter, she could fetch it after seeing Antonio. His sense of decency would not be offended by her hair being uncovered.

'I will be home by early afternoon,' she said. 'Don't get into trouble.'

Although her grief for her father felt like a stone on her chest – always there, stealing her breath from her – Ana felt her spirits lift as she set off back up the mountain.

She walked through their vineyards, nodding to the labourers working on the vines. During the night, she'd wondered if the men who had visited the house yesterday had come for money. Ana would not be able to bear it if they had to sell the family land, but the fact was they'd have trouble paying their bills at the end of the next quarter. They needed this year's yield of grapes to be good.

She tried to put everything from her mind as she began to climb the mountain. Higher and higher, keeping a steady pace, her boots pounding the dry earth. The slope got steeper. The surface was a mixture of gravel and stone and Ana's boots kept slipping, but she kept going.

She had lived her whole life in this landscape. Ana knew the changing colours of the seasons. She knew the smells and the sounds as well as she knew her own face in the mirror. But today there seemed to be mounds where before the land had been flat, strange hollow dips where before it had been level. Nothing looked quite the same.

The sky was a wide expanse of white and there was an odd glow as if a sea fog had settled over the summit. The air was humid for the time of day, though there was no sign of a storm. Grey clouds were covering the highest peaks of the Black Mountain. They looked almost like steam from boiling water.

Ana frowned. If her father had been here, she could have asked him what it meant. As a farmer, he was always alert to any change in the weather. She would have asked him too about the tremor she had felt yesterday.

'It is just the earth letting us know who is in charge,' he'd have said, as he always did, and Ana would have been reassured. 'The earth is reminding us to take good care of her.'

Chapter Eight

Like Ana, widow Silva had not slept.

At dawn, she gave up and came to her usual place by the fishing racks. Her thoughts were buzzing in her head like wasps in a jar. She feared there was a link between the changes on the mountain and the death of Ana's father, Tomas Perez. She didn't want to admit it, but she was scared.

Some time later, she was drinking a third cup of bitter, black coffee when she saw the tall, thin figure of Antonio coming down the sloping street to the port.

'Thank God,' she said.

She pulled herself to her feet, sending her cup flying to the ground. The hot coffee hissed and spat on the fire. She took no notice, just walked as quickly as her old legs would carry her across the sand to meet him.

'Something is happening,' she said when he drew level.

Antonio nodded. 'All the signs are there, yes.'

The two old friends turned and looked over the spire of the church of Saint Ana, to the Black Mountain beyond. Clouds of dark grey smoke could be seen hovering above the crater.

'Is that how it began before?'

Again, he nodded. 'First, the tremors, then white clouds of ash, then grey clouds, then the sky turned red. Black ash and lava burst up from three craters. A river of fire, killing everything and turning the land to rock.'

The old woman looked at him. 'Tomas Perez saw what was coming?'

'He was worried about several things. But he saw the changes on the mountain before I did.'

She tilted her head. 'And now he's dead.'

'Now he's dead.' Antonio held her gaze. 'They do not want anything to threaten their wealth.'

For a moment, the two old people stood in silence. Antonio did not want to tell her more, for fear of putting her in danger. He had no doubt his friend, Tomas Perez, had been killed to stop him talking.

'How long do you think?' widow Silva asked.

Antonio let his arms drop by his side. 'Nothing is certain. The Black Mountain has complained before, but then settled back to sleep.'

She looked at him with her fading eyes. 'But if it does not?'

'Two days, perhaps three at the most,' he said.

Widow Silva made the sign of the cross. 'What can we do?'

Antonio put his thin hand on her shoulder. 'There's nothing anyone can do to stop it. But we must warn everyone in the town. People must prepare to leave.'

They both looked along the narrow street up to where the town hall stood. It was an imposing white building at the heart of the main square. A colourful flag fluttered from its pole. Bright flowers in wooden window boxes lined the first-floor windows. It looked splendid and spoke of the importance of the town as Tenerife's biggest trading port.

'But will they listen?' widow Silva said quietly.

Antonio's weathered face fell. 'They did not listen to Tomas and I do not think they will listen to me,' he said, 'but we have no choice but to try.'

Chapter Nine

'Antonio,' Ana called.

Straight away, she could tell he wasn't at home. There was a quality of silence and of stillness that spoke of a place abandoned. There wasn't a breath of air, not a single sound. Not even the scuttle of lizards in the undergrowth. It was as if the world had stopped.

'Antonio?' she said again, all the same.

The door to the wooden shack stood wide and the shutters of the window were open. Had something happened to call him away?

Ana walked across the small patch of barren land in front of the shack. She bent down and held her hand over the fire. The ash was cold. It had died some time ago. A few burnt pieces of wood lay scattered and a cast-iron cooking pot was sitting in the dust.

'Antonio?' she said for a third time, this time in a whisper.

Her heart thudding, Ana moved slowly towards the tiny building. She took a deep breath, then looked inside. To her relief, Antonio wasn't there. After her father's death, she realised she was nervous about what she might find.

The shack was small and basic, just a single room with a sleeping platform upstairs, but it was clean. She looked around. Everything looked as usual. There was a wooden bowl on the table with a loaf of bread beneath a cloth. A plate and a wooden cup. She picked it up and smelt the dregs of some local wine – their wine, perhaps?

Ana frowned. Antonio said he had nothing worth stealing, but he always locked his door and shuttered his window if he was going down to the town. Then again, there were no signs that he had left in a hurry.

She heard a sound. A low bleating.

Ana ran round to the back of the building, where she found Antonio's nanny goat. It was tied to a wooden post by a long harness. There were a few vegetable tops in the feeding manger and a dew pond within reach for water. All the same, Ana could see the goat needed milking. It wasn't like Antonio to fail to look after his animals.

Still wondering where he had gone, Ana fetched the low, three-legged stool and the metal pail. The pail was dusty inside with a kind of fine white ash. She turned it upside down and wiped it out with her hand. The ash had a slippery feel and, when she brought her fingers close to her face, there was a sharp smell, like burnt lemons.

She wiped it clean with the hem of her skirt, then began. Leaning her face against the goat's warm fur, Ana massaged its udders to collect the milk in the bucket. Its coat was wiry and prickled her cheek. Once or twice, she thought she felt a slight tremor beneath her feet, but the goat was calm and that, in turn, soothed her.

When she was done, Ana stretched her shoulders and flexed her fingers. At least Antonio would have milk for his supper when he came back.

Then she noticed something strange. It must be a trick of the light.

Ana went over to the pond. The water had turned grey, as if dye had been poured into it. She dipped her hand in and, straight away, her skin began to itch. And there was that same smell of bad eggs, but much worse.

Then, suddenly, Ana felt the ground jolt beneath her feet. It gave a violent lurch, just like yesterday, only this time it lasted longer. It was as if she was on the deck of a ship rolling and swaying on the sea. She braced her knees, so as not to fall. Now she could feel something on the back of her neck too. Rain? She looked up and saw that a light grey ash had started to fall.

Just as quickly as it had begun, the earth stopped shaking. The ground was stable, as if nothing had happened. But the ash kept falling. Another of her father's sayings came to mind. This time, the memory did not reassure her.

'There is no need to be afraid of the mountain until the black snow comes,' he would say.

Not snow, of course, but ash. Grey ash was coming from the crater of the Black Mountain. And, after the grey ash, would come the black snow.

Ana knew that this was more serious than anything she had ever known. She had to warn the town about what was happening on the mountain before it was too late. Then it came to her that must be where Antonio had gone. He had seen the danger and gone to raise the alarm.

She ran back into the shack. She found paper and a piece of charcoal, and wrote a note explaining what had happened. She added that she needed to speak to him about her father's letter. Then she put the note under his wooden cup on the table and left.

Ana didn't want to leave the goat, so she

decided to take it with her. Her mother could look after it. Although her mother found talking with people difficult, she had a gentle hand with animals. Ana untied the goat, hooked the rope over her arm and led it quickly down the mountain.

And all the time, Ana could feel the ground complaining beneath her feet.

Chapter Ten

'Boo!'

Rudi jumped out of his skin. The twins laughed.

'Why did you do that?' Rudi shouted, his face red. He stood up from behind the fishing boat and brushed the sand from his breeches.

'Why were you hiding?' Pablo said.

'I'm watching widow Silva's smoking racks. I have every right to be here. Leave me alone.'

Rudi was two years older than the twins, but they always treated him like a kid. Determined not to cry, he turned away.

'Don't be like that,' Pablo said, putting his hand on Rudi's shoulder.

'Come down to the port with us,' Carlos added.

Rudi shrugged off Pablo's arm. 'I have to stay here.'

Pablo looked around. 'No one will know.'

'I have to stay here,' Rudi said again.

'Where is widow Silva anyhow?' asked Carlos.

Though Rudi did not like the Perez twins, he

could not resist showing he knew something that they did not.

'She went with Antonio.'

Pablo's eyebrows shot up in surprise. 'The old man from the mountain?'

'The same.'

'What's he doing down in the town?' Carlos asked.

Rudi shrugged. 'All I know is that widow Silva sent a message to him yesterday, and today he came.'

Pablo grabbed his withered arm. Through his thin shirt, Rudi felt Pablo's strong fingers pressing too hard.

'Was it about my father?' Pablo said in a low voice.

'I don't know.'

Rudi tried to pull away, but Pablo only held on tighter. 'Where have they gone?'

'They went towards the town hall,' Rudi said. Then, in a moment of courage, he added: 'It's to do with the mountain. Not your father.'

All three boys looked up to the layer of clouds above the summit of the Black Mountain. It was now a dark grey. Rudi felt the pressure on his arm released.

'When widow Silva comes back,' Pablo said,

as if nothing had happened, 'ask her to save four fish for us. Ana sent us to get them.'

Rudi rubbed his arm with his good hand, wishing he was brave enough to fight Pablo. But there were two of them and only one of him and, besides, Ana wouldn't like it. He wished he had a sister like Ana, someone to care for him.

'All right,' he said in a quiet voice.

He had lost again. But one day he'd show them. He'd show them all.

Chapter Eleven

'Mama!' Ana called from the back garden as she arrived home. 'I'm back.'

'Ah, Miss Perez. Come in.'

A man's voice. It was an order not a request.

Feeling nervous, Ana tied up the goat and washed her hands under the pump. She knew she looked a sight. Her woollen skirt was stained, her white chemise was caked with dust and her head was uncovered. On impulse, she pushed her father's letter into his leather bag and left it outside. Then, she twisted her hair into a plait and stepped into their main room.

A square room with white walls and wooden beams, it served as a living space and kitchen. There was a brick open fire with a black kettle hanging above it. Brass pots and pans were set on a dresser, with wooden bowls, plates and linen beneath. In the middle of the room there was a large table, worn and scratched from years of use, and six ladder-backed chairs. On the wall was a wooden cross.

'Mama?' Ana said.

She glanced at her mother. She was sitting beside the cold fire holding her prayer beads. Her face was hidden behind her black widow's veil. When Ana bent down and kissed her on the cheek, she was aware that two men were standing in the shadows beside the front door.

'These gentlemen want to talk to you,' her mother said in a timid voice.

Ana felt the hairs on the back of her neck stand on end.

The visitors were not farmers like them, but important men. Powerful men. She turned as first the priest, then his brother – the mayor himself – stepped into the light.

Her mother pushed her forward. 'Greet our guests, Ana.'

The priest, fat and sweating in the heat, held out his hand. His fingernails were dirty. To please her mother, Ana forced herself to kneel and kiss his ring. Everything about the mayor boasted of his wealth and importance. He wore a long golden jacket, with black silk thread, red breeches, white garters and square-toed shoes. He looked like a nobleman from Spain. His wig, made from real human hair, was a mass of black curls; it was parted in the middle and held in place by flour paste. Ana could see drips of flour sliding down his forehead.

Ana gave a brief bow. 'What might I do for you, sir?'

The mayor clicked his fingers.

The priest stepped forward. 'It has come to our notice that you have buried your father,' he said.

Ana held her nerve. 'Yesterday, yes.'

'Did you get permission for this act?'

Ana felt her stomach lurch. 'The grave is on our land, and since it was not permitted to bury him in holy ground . . .'

'That is God's law,' the priest said.

The mayor held up his hand. 'Ah, your land,' he said. 'That, I fear, is the problem, Miss Perez. The land was in your father's name.'

Ana held her breath. 'I do not understand, sir.'

He gave a thin smile. 'Oh, I'm sure you do. A clever girl like you.'

'You flatter me,' she said, forcing herself to meet his gaze.

'That was not what my brother intended,' the priest said sharply. 'You must be respectful.'

The mayor laughed. It was a hollow, ugly sound. 'You know, as well as I do, that a woman cannot own land,' he said.

'Exceptions are made,' Ana said. 'My mother

is only holding the land in trust until my brothers come of age.'

'Which will not be for four years.'

They stared at one another. The mayor could allow her mother to keep the land – most widows were allowed to do so – but Ana knew they couldn't raise the money for a bribe. If, indeed, that was what he wanted.

From behind his back, the mayor produced her straw hat. Ana's eyes widened with surprise.

'Is this yours?' he said.

Ana pretended to look. 'It might well be, sir. I mislaid mine some days past.'

'Where?' The word was quick and sharp.

Ana wasn't sure what this was about, but she kept her voice steady. She didn't want to give anything away.

'In my grief for my father, I have been walking on the lower slopes by our vines. To clear my head. I must have dropped it then.'

The mayor narrowed his eyes. 'Not higher up the mountain?'

Now she understood. His men must have found it in the clearing and, for some reason, that bothered him. But why? Ana glanced at her mother and could hear she was moving her prayer beads.

'No, sir,' Ana said. 'I need to stay close to home. To be on hand for my mother when she needs me.'

'The suicide letter your father left,' he said, changing tack. 'Do you still have it?'

Ana felt her legs start to shake, but she stood firm. 'I do not, sir,' she lied. 'I burnt it to spare my mother pain.'

The mayor looked at her for a moment longer, then placed the hat upon the table.

'Some days before your father took his life, he was heard talking wildly. Causing trouble.'

Ana heard her mother shift in her chair.

'Indeed, spreading lies,' the mayor carried on. 'Telling people to leave the town. Claiming the Black Mountain was going to erupt. It was very bad for trade. If ships do not come, the whole island will suffer.'

'But what if he was right?' she cried, before she could stop herself. 'All the signs are there. We have to warn people.'

The mayor pointed his finger at her. 'It would be a mistake for you to repeat these lies, Miss Perez. Especially while the matter of your land is under discussion.'

Now, Ana understood. It wasn't money he wanted but her silence. The mayor would let them stay so long as she said nothing. She was to keep silent about her father's death and the changes on the mountain.

'Do you understand?' he said.

Ana raised her chin and stared him in the eye. 'Yes. I understand.'

Her mother, realising a deal had been struck, grasped the priest's hand.

'Bless you, Father. Thank you, thank you.'

The priest placed his greasy hand on Mrs Perez's head. 'The Lord takes care of those who serve him well,' he said. 'I will pray for you.' He glanced at Ana. 'I will pray for you all.'

Chapter Twelve

After the two men had gone, Ana thought her legs might give way.

She was scared, yes, but mostly she was angry. Already, she was going over things in her mind. She regretted not defending her father, but she knew she had no choice if they were not to be turned off their land.

'I'm sorry,' her mother sobbed. 'I could not stop them coming in.'

'It's not your fault, Mama,' Ana said, putting her arm around her mother's shoulders. 'None of this is your fault.'

Ana picked up her hat.

'Where are you going?' her mother said in a panic.

'To the port to fetch Pablo and Carlos. I will send them to sit with you while I find Antonio.'

Her mother shook her head. 'No, no. The trouble began when your father started to listen to Antonio. He brings this family bad luck.'

Ana knelt down and took her mother's hands in hers. 'If Papa and Antonio are right – and I think they are – it doesn't matter what the priest thinks, or what the mayor says. If the Black Mountain erupts, then everything will be swept away. Our land, this house, even the town. We have to do something.'

'It's never happened,' her mother cried. 'Your father was always talking about the mountain erupting, but it never happened. He was wrong.'

Ana kissed her mother. 'I will be back as soon as I can.'

A large crowd was gathering at the steps of the town hall. Fishermen, housewives with their baskets full of shopping, tradesmen, children playing with wooden hoops in the street. A few sailors, just off the boats bound for the colonies, chattered in Dutch and English. Ana wondered what was happening.

As she walked into the square, she saw her brothers, Pablo and Carlos, sitting watching from the wall beside the church. Poor Rudi was standing a little way apart. She waved to attract their attention, but none of the boys noticed. Then she saw widow Silva at the front of the crowd and went to join her.

'Have you seen Antonio?' Ana asked. 'I need to speak to him. It is urgent.'

'You'll have to wait,' widow Silva said, pointing to where the gaunt figure dressed in a black long-coat and breeches was climbing the steps to the front of the town hall. 'He's going to speak.'

Ana pulled her father's letter from her pocket and showed it to the older woman. 'Can you see these six letters?'

Widow Silva shook her head. 'They mean nothing to me.'

Ana pointed. 'Do you see now? If you put them in order? B – L – A – N – C – A.'

The old woman peered, then nodded. 'Yes.'

'You see now how my father hid the name?' Ana said, tapping the letter. 'I think this is why my father was killed. I think he saw something from the mountain.' She paused. 'The mayor and the priest came to the house earlier asking for the letter.'

Widow Silva's eyes widened with shock. 'You must be careful, Ana.'

The chance of saying more was lost. Antonio had reached the top of the steps and he was clapping his hands to get the crowd's attention.

'Friends, will you listen to me?'

The crowd shuffled on their feet.

'Friends, fellow islanders,' Antonio tried again. 'Will you hear me?'

A bearded man at the front shouted out. 'Let's hear what he has to say.'

A hush went around the crowd. One by one, people fell silent.

'Thank you,' Antonio said, raising his voice so those at the back could hear him too. 'Friends, it pains me to say this, but we are in danger.'

'Only from Spanish taxes!' someone joked.

Antonio carried on. 'We live in the shadow of the Black Mountain.'

'We know that!' shouted the butcher's boy, and everyone laughed.

'For years it has protected us,' Antonio went on. 'It has given us good soil to grow our vegetables and fruit. Our vines. We have not suffered like those in other parts of the island have suffered.'

'And long may it last!' the bearded man said.

Antonio spread out his arms. Ana thought he looked like a preacher and felt the crowd react.

'Things are changing,' he said. 'I live on the Black Mountain. For weeks, now, I have kept watch – noticing how the plants are growing, how the animals are living, how the air is different. The land itself is unsteady. There have been tremors.'

'There are always tremors,' the butcher's boy called out.

'That's just you when you've had too much ale on a Saturday night,' his friend jeered, and the crowd cheered.

Antonio raised his voice. 'What you say is true, my friend. There have always been tremors. Nature changes with the seasons. We all know this.' He turned to look at the Black Mountain, then back to face the crowd. 'But this time is different. Our masters, who run this town, know this. There have been many reports and from different people. But they are telling you otherwise. They say there is no danger, but they are wrong.'

'Don't believe a word of it!' a red-faced man shouted.

Ana knew him as one of the most faithful of the priest's followers. A wealthy tailor, he was always the first to point out wrong-doing. He spoke badly of women who went out with their hair uncovered, or men who drank too much, or children who would not sit still in church. Pablo had more than once felt the back of his hand.

'Do you deny the evidence of your own eyes?' Antonio said. 'Can you not see the grey ash? Can you not see the grey clouds above the crater? The men who rule this town know we are in danger. It is their greed that makes them deny what is happening.'

'We've seen changes like this before,' the tailor said, crossing his arms. 'Nothing happens. You'll ruin our business if you keep on like this. The mayor is right to protect our trade. Our town is rich because of him.'

Ana could see Antonio was losing the attention of the crowd.

'My friends,' Antonio said, raising his voice to be heard, 'put away as much water as you can and store it, reserve it. Wherever ash comes down, there will be no water to drink. Turn your boats upside down or they will be filled up with ash.'

'You won't scare us!'

'When the Black Mountain erupts,' Antonio said, 'there will be little time.'

'If it erupts!'

Ana looked at Antonio standing on his own – a gaunt black figure – then at the mass of men and women standing in front of her at the foot of the steps.

'We must listen to him,' she cried, from the back of the crowd. 'He has seen such things with his own eyes. He knows what he is talking about!'

Widow Silva gave her support. 'Yes, let him finish. I want to hear what he saw.'

Ana saw the tailor shaking his head in disgust, but most people became quiet again.

'It was in the north-east of the island,' Antonio began. 'Some two years ago. Like us, they had grown used to their mountains tremors. Like us, they did not expect things to change. It was an ordinary morning, like this one. A white sky, bright sunshine behind the clouds, no wind. That's when the volcano started snowing, a fine dust, then heavier. It's called pumice, a sort of burnt stone. But not burnt black. It's white and it chokes you if it gets in your mouth and nose.'

'The mountain often sends up white dust,' a woman said.

Antonio carried on. 'It started as dust, then it was thicker, the size of grains of wheat or rice. Then the noise started, lots of noise, explosions like the firing of a canon, but under the earth. Then bigger pieces started falling from the sky, as big as a man's fist. If you were unlucky, they broke the tiles on your roof. The animals all started trying to escape from their pens. They knew.'

Ana could sense the crowd was growing too restless. She willed Antonio to keep going.

'Next came the dark,' Antonio cried. 'It didn't happen all at once, but slowly, slowly, the sky filled up with ash and the sun grew dim until there was no more sun. You couldn't see your hand in front of your face. Some people hid inside their houses. Others ran for their boats. Others knelt in the streets and prayed or wept. Last, came a noise like the end of the world and the mountain blew open. Fire started to run down the slopes, rolling fire, like a slow river, but red-hot rock.'

For a moment, there was silence. In the distance, they could hear the gulls and seabirds at the port.

Then, suddenly, everyone started talking, shouting, arguing at once. Too many voices filling the air.

'The north-east is different from here.'

'That could never happen to us. The Black Mountain is always sleeping.'

'You are making it up!'

'In the north-east, they said the same,' Antonio shouted, struggling to make himself heard. 'But a river of fire flowed down the valley towards the town. It killed everyone, both those who feared the mountain and those who believed there was no danger. That town doesn't exist any more. The river of fire swept it, burning, into the sea.'

'You have no evidence things are changing,'

the tailor called out from the back of the crowd. He had now gathered more people to his side.

Before she had time to think what would happen if she spoke out, Ana heard herself shout. 'He does.'

She felt people turning round to look at her.

'I've seen it with my own eyes too. The tremors are stronger on the mountain. They last longer. The water is poisoned, the land is over-heating. Antonio has evidence . . .' She paused. 'As did my father.'

'Your father was a coward and a sinner,' the tailor shouted.

Ana watched Pablo launch himself off the wall, followed by Carlos. In a split second, Ana saw everything like a painting of what was happening: widow Silva's worried face, Antonio's thin black figure on the steps and then, on all sides of the square, the mayor's soldiers coming to break up the crowd.

Ana was at a crossroads. She either had to put her family above all else, and hold her tongue, or do what she knew was right. Despite what might happen, Ana knew she had to continue her father's work. It was what he would have wanted.

'Take this,' she said, pushing her father's letter

into widow Silva's hands. Then she stepped forward.

'My father was killed to stop him speaking out,' Ana shouted. 'We must leave. Before it's too late.'

Ana felt two rough hands grab her and she was pulled backwards off her feet. Pablo and Carlos flew at the soldiers, but they were batted away like flies.

'Let her go!' shouted Rudi, trying to hold on to her arm. Seconds later, he too was lying on the ground with blood seeping from his lip.

The crowd was now surrounded. The soldiers took aim with their guns, forbidding anyone to resist.

'Go home!' they commanded. 'By order of the mayor. Anyone who stays will also be arrested.'

Ana was dragged up the steps into the town hall. She saw Antonio had been arrested too. Both his arms were pulled up behind his back and his nose was bleeding. But Ana knew they had done the right thing. They had tried to warn the town. Yes, they had silenced her father, they had tried to bully her. But she had fought back.

As they pulled her inside, she heard the church bell begin to ring for Vespers.

Chapter Thirteen

'What shall we do?' Carlos said.

He looked at his brother. Pablo always knew what do to. But he said nothing.

'I have an idea,' said Rudi.

'You! As if you're any use!' Pablo said.

For once, Rudi did not back down. 'Do you have a plan?'

He started at Pablo and, this time, it was Pablo who looked away.

'Go on,' said Carlos. He sounded scared.

'There is a way into the town hall through the church,' Rudi said. 'We could find out where Ana is being held and then, well . . .'

'What, get her out! That's stupid—' Pablo said, but Carlos was listening.

'Please will you show us?' he said.

Rudi didn't smile. He didn't want to be like Pablo. Always making fun and thinking he was better than everyone else. But maybe Carlos wasn't so bad. His heart was singing that Carlos seemed to trust him.

In the distance, there was a rumble. It sounded like thunder, but the boys weren't sure any more. Antonio's words had frightened them. The grey clouds above the mountain were turning black. Each of them thought they felt the ground shift, but they said nothing. They didn't want to lose face in front of the others.

'We'll have to wait until after Vespers is over and everyone's retired for the night,' Rudi said. 'Then I'll show you.'

The light was beginning to fade from the sky. Widow Silva had waited until the last of the soldiers on patrol had left the square before going to find Ana's mother.

Keeping to the shadows, widow Silva hurried through the back streets of the town and up the slope towards the Perez land. By seven o'clock, she was knocking on the back door of their house.

'Mrs Perez?' she called. 'May I come in?'

There was no sound.

Widow Silva believed in the old ways of the island. Good manners, not going into another woman's house without being invited. But these were not normal times.

With a bad feeling, she turned the handle and

went inside. The room was in shadow with both the windows shuttered, despite the humid evening. There was an odd buzzing – flies, she realised – then her heart started to beat faster. She could sense something was wrong.

'Mrs Perez, are you here?'

Then her hand flew to her mouth.

'Lord have mercy,' she whispered, crossing herself.

At her eye level, a pair of black boots was spinning slowly, the toes pointing down to the tiled floor. A body was hanging in the still air. Mrs Perez was dead, her pale hands limp by her side. Widow Silva forced herself to look up. A thick yard of rope had been thrown over the wooden beam. Her head was twisted to one side where her neck had broken, but her face was hidden by her veil. Widow Silva was grateful to be spared that sight at least.

It looked as if Mrs Perez had taken her own life too. Was that so surprising? She had struggled to cope after the death of her husband. Widow Silva looked around for a note, but there was nothing.

Then, she thought again. For all the loss and tragedy in her life, Mrs Perez had never lost her Catholic faith. However hard things were, she would never have killed herself. For her, it would have been a mortal sin. It would have cast her out of Heaven.

But there was more than just that. Widow Silva could see they had made a mistake. Every one of the six chairs was set around the kitchen table. If Mrs Perez had hanged herself, she would have had to stand on a chair and kick it away from under her.

Widow Silva's hand went to the pocket of her apron. Ana had thrust her father's letter at her as the soldiers approached. It was clear she had been right to do so. Ana's suspicions were right. This was murder. Both Ana's parents had been killed. First her father and now her mother.

But what precisely had Tomas Perez seen? What did they think he might have told his wife?

Widow Silva muttered a prayer and crossed herself again. She hated to leave Mrs Perez as she was, but she had to get help. She could not cut down the body on her own. Leaving everything as she had found it, widow Silva left the same way she had come. After she had laid Mrs Perez out, she'd have to find a way to speak to Antonio. Wherever they had taken him. And then, God help her, she would have to find Ana and tell her that her mother was dead.

She turned cold. What if something had happened to Ana too?

In the distance above the mountain, a cloud of black ash belched into the still air. Widow Silva glanced up. They were running out of time. She hurried on.

Rudi, Carlos and Pablo sat in silence in the alleyway that ran behind the church listening to the people leaving after Vespers. For an hour they had hardly spoken.

As soon as he was sure the way was clear, Rudi stood up and signalled for Pablo and Carlos to follow. Rudi was surprised – and pleased – that they did what he said without complaint. The three boys crept into the church, each of them nervous but trying to hide it. Rudi's eyes darted to left and right, making sure the priest wasn't still there. But the nave was empty and the air silent. Just a smell of incense remained.

Rudi led them to the side chapel. There was a special altar where people prayed for fishermen and sailors with statues of Saint Francis and Saint Nicolas. Behind the altar was a small, quiet space, just big enough to hide in when the world was unkind. Rudi often hid there.

Beyond that, a small wooden door.

'It was put here for the priest in the old days,' Rudi said, 'so he could go between the church and the town hall without anyone seeing him. It leads into the private garden at the back of the building. There are never any guards there.'

The three boys looked at the wooden door.

'We can hide in the gardens until it's dark. They are private. No one goes in there.'

'And then what?' hissed Pablo, finding a little of his old spirit. 'What are we going to do?'

Rudi looked him in the eye. 'We will save Ana. And Antonio too.'

Wednesday, 5 May 1706

The day of the eruption

Chapter Fourteen

Ana was being held prisoner on the first floor of the town hall.

She had been brought here from the town square hours ago. They had searched her and locked her in, but she was unharmed. They seemed to have forgotten about her. She had counted the hours by the tolling of the church bell. Now it was dark, though thin shafts of moonlight shone through the wooden shutters.

She could hear the Black Mountain rumbling in the distance.

To start with, Ana had paced up and down, the boards creaking beneath her feet. She was putting the pieces of the puzzle together in her mind. She was angry, then scared. She was thirsty and she was hungry. Now she was simply tired.

She hated to think of her mother and brothers in their little white house, not knowing what was happening to her. She hoped widow Silva had gone to sit with them. Ana remembered the blood on Antonio's face and hoped he was all right. The soldiers hadn't hurt her, but she feared they would be less kind to him. Was he also being held in the town hall? Or had they taken him to the prison at the port?

Ana heard the bells strike for ten o'clock.

At least, in these long hours alone, she'd had time to work out both how and why her father had been murdered. The 'how' was simple. She guessed he had been knocked out first. After that, it would have been easy for two men to stage his death to look like suicide. She did not think the mayor himself would have done this, but she was certain now it was on his orders.

The 'why' was harder, but she thought she had worked it out too. It wasn't because of his warnings about the Black Mountain. Rather, it was because, during his visits to the crater to look at the changes, her father had seen something he should not have seen. That made most sense. The attack on their vines, the rumours about their money troubles, his murder – all came because he had been on the mountain at the wrong moment.

From so high up, her father would have been able to see what was happening in the town. But also what was happening out at sea. His eye glass and his leather bag had been found with his body. For the name her father had hidden in his letter was not the name of a person, but of a ship. A ship that had gone down off the north-west coast of Tenerife in January.

Last January, when the worst of the winter storms came blowing in off the Atlantic, *La Blanca* had gone down not far from the port. Every man on board had drowned. The treasure had gone down with the ship.

The White Ship – La Blanca – had been one of Spain's most important ships, carrying silver and pearls, silk and spices. The ship had five masts with billowing white sails. The red and gold flag of royal Spain fluttered at her stern. It was part of the treasure fleet of the Spanish king. Several fighting ships had sailed with her to protect the priceless cargo – gold bullion, jewels, precious goods all bound for their homeland in the east.

On the following day, when the weather cleared a little, the mayor had sent a rescue mission out into the rough seas. The port itself was protected by a high harbour wall. By order of the mayor, no one had been allowed on the wall that day. The waves were too high, the sea too wild. At least, that was the reason given. Ana now realised it was so that no one could see what the rescue mission was doing.

The mission recovered nothing.

A week later, the mayor held a meeting in the town hall to report. He failed to explain why the ship had sunk – she was well built – and she hadn't been blown onto the rocks. There were no enemy vessels in the area. No one could explain the loss of the ship and the entire crew.

Now, Ana couldn't believe how blind she'd been.

Nothing could be seen from the beach – the harbour wall was in the way. But if her father had been high up on the mountain that day in January, he might have seen something. He always had his eye glass with him. He could have seen what had happened to the ship. And the treasure.

It was after the sinking that her father had changed. He had taken to asking questions at the port and in the town about *La Blanca*. Not long afterwards had come the attack on their vines, then the rumours that they were in debt.

Then suddenly, in the quiet of her prison room, Ana heard a sound. A tapping sound. She leapt to her feet. Were the soldiers finally coming back?

She heard the noise again and realised it was coming from outside the window. She crept across the room.

'Who's there?'

'It's me.'

She recognised the voice. 'Carlos!'

'Can you open the shutters?' he whispered.

Ana pushed them open and peered out into the dark. She could just make out the top of her brother's head. He was balanced on a narrow ledge below the sill. Below was the private garden at the rear of the town hall.

'How did you climb up? It's so high.'

'It's not so hard,' Carlos said, though his voice was tight from the effort.

'Where's Pablo?' she asked.

'He's with Rudi, trying to find Antonio. We heard the guards talking. Antonio's not being held here. They took him to the prison at the port.' He paused. 'Can you climb out?'

Ana looked down. Before, she would never have gone against the mayor and the laws of the town. But things were different now.

'I don't know,' Ana said.

In the distance, there was a loud rumble of noise. Like dry thunder.

'I hate that noise,' Carlos said. He sounded

77

very young, and very afraid. 'It's like the sound of canon fire.'

Ana could see how the sky above the Black Mountain was glowing red. A huge red gash in the clouds. They were running out of time.

'I'm coming.'

Ana tucked her long skirt into her under-clothes and took a deep breath. Then she swung her leg over the sill and lowered herself onto the ledge.

Chapter Fifteen

Antonio did not know how much longer he could last against their blows and their questions.

He was in the jail at the port. His ordeal had begun when it was light and now it was dark. He had no sense of day or night any more. There was just pain and the brief gaps between pain. His left eye was swollen shut and there was a taste of blood in his mouth. His nose was broken and several of his teeth were loose.

Antonio felt his head being jerked back.

'I will ask you one last time. What did Tomas Perez tell you?'

Antonio struggled to speak. 'He told me nothing.'

He braced himself for another blow. He was tied to a chair, his arms strapped to the wooden struts. This time, the fist drove into his belly. He grunted in pain.

'You are aware that we are holding Miss Perez too?' the man said.

Antonio had become used to the voice. It wasn't the mayor himself, though he had no doubt he was nearby. It was one of his right-hand men. Antonio could smell his long leather coat. Beneath his blindfold, he could see the soldier's boots.

'She's just a girl,' he said quickly.

'She's sixteen. Old enough.' Antonio felt the man's face come closer. 'It's well known that her father trusted her.'

'On my life, Perez told her nothing.'

Antonio felt the man draw back. 'You will forgive me if I don't take your word for that.'

He heard whispering, then he heard the voice of the mayor.

'Bring the girl here,' he said, 'and we will see what she knows.'

'No!' Antonio struggled on the chair to get free. Then, to his horror, he heard footsteps crossing the room and the soldiers laughing. 'No, leave her alone.'

Ana held on to the ledge with her fingers and lowered herself as close as she could to the ground. She needed to be brave and let herself drop the last few feet.

'It's only the height of a man,' Carlos whispered up at her.

Ana counted to three, then let go. For a moment, she was falling. Then, she felt a jolt in her ankles and she fell sideways.

'There,' Carlos said, helping her to her feet. 'That wasn't so bad.'

'You are braver than I am,' Ana said, taking his hand. 'I must go to Mama. She will be frightened.'

'Widow Silva said she would go and sit with her,' Carlos said. 'It was Rudi's idea.'

Ana sighed with relief. 'Good. We will fetch them both as soon as we've freed Antonio.'

There was another rumble from the Black Mountain. The tiny explosions were happening closer together. Ana heard Carlos catch his breath.

'Ana, what are we going to do?'

'Find the others,' she said.

'No,' he said in a small voice. 'I mean, if the mountain erupts.'

They both looked up. The night sky was glowing even more fiercely around the crater. The sounds of tiny explosions were happening more often.

Ana took her brother's hand. 'Let's find the others.'

Chapter Sixteen

Antonio was alone in his cell, although there were soldiers on guard outside the door.

He struggled to loosen the rope tying his hands, but it was no good. He was desperate. Antonio did not fear death, but he had promised Tomas Perez he would protect the family if anything happened to him.

He had failed.

Through the bars of the window, he heard an even louder rumble, like a crack of thunder right overhead. Even during his ordeal, Antonio had realised the sounds coming from the mountain were getting closer together. It wouldn't be long now.

Antonio's shoulders slumped. He had failed in this too.

He had done his best to warn the town of the danger, but they hadn't listened. They were too comfortable in their fine houses and beautiful clothes, with the wealth the trading ships brought into port. They didn't believe the Black

Mountain would turn on them after all these years living safely in its shadow.

Suddenly, he heard a scuffling sound behind him. A soft thud. Though his eyes were still blindfolded and it was dark, he could sense someone – or something – was now in the cell with him. Was it a rat? The jail, like the port itself, was over-run with rats.

'Who's there?' he said in a low voice. Then he wondered if this had been the plan all along. Perhaps they had left him alone so that someone could slip inside and kill him.

Antonio braced himself, half expecting to feel a knife at his throat. Instead, he felt his ties loosen and the blindfold being pulled from his eyes.

All the same, Antonio jumped up from the chair, ready to defend himself.

'Don't hurt me!' Rudi cried.

Antonio stared in disbelief. 'In the Lord's name, how did you get in here?'

Rudi pointed up to the high window. 'Pablo lifted me up and I slipped through the bars.'

Antonio was speechless. Rudi was small and very thin, but even so it was amazing the boy had fitted through.

'Rudi, you can't stay. They will punish you

if they find you here. I don't want that on my conscience.' He glanced up again at the window. 'There's no way I can get out that way.'

Rudi took no notice. 'There are only two guards outside,' he said. 'We have to get them to open the door. Pablo will do something to draw them away.'

Antonio looked at the ragged child. Rudi was always on his own, always left out of the other boys' games. But tonight he seemed to have grown more bold. Antonio didn't think there was a hope that the plan would work, but he was touched by the boy's efforts to help.

'Very well,' he said.

Antonio looked around the cell. The only thing he could use as a weapon was the chair itself. 'Stand behind the door.'

Once Rudi was in position, Antonio began to bang the chair against the floor, trying to loosen the legs. He started shouting.

'Hey!' he yelled. 'Guards!'

From the other side of the door, he heard the soldiers. One banged on the door with the butt of his rifle.

'Quiet in there.'

Antonio took no notice; he just kept banging the chair against the wall and the floor and shouting. A leg came loose, which he passed to Rudi as a weapon.

'Go for his knees,' he said.

Rudi nodded.

'Hey, fools!' Antonio shouted again. 'Idiots! You are standing out there all night, when the mayor's tucked up in bed. He won't come back until morning, yet you're still here.'

'Be quiet, I tell you!'

Antonio kept up the noise until, at last, he heard the sound of the key being turned in the lock. He nodded at Rudi, who got ready holding the piece of broken wood in his good hand.

At the moment the door started to open, they heard one of the soldiers shout.

'Who's throwing things?'

Then they heard Pablo's voice outside. 'You can't catch me!'

'Come here!' one of the soldiers yelled in anger.

Antonio heard the sound of one set of boots running and prayed that Pablo was faster than the soldier. Hoping to take the second soldier by surprise, Antonio suddenly tugged the door open. The soldier half fell into the cell. Rudi took aim and smashed the wood into his kneecap.

The soldier shouted as Antonio brought the

chair down on his head, knocking him out. He grabbed him under the shoulders and dragged him into the cell, then man and boy slipped out and locked the door behind them. Antonio put the key in his pocket and slapped Rudi on the back.

'You did well.'

From outside, they heard a shot. Antonio looked grim.

'Pablo!' Rudi said, and started to run as fast as his damaged foot would let him.

Chapter Seventeen

It had taken widow Silva a long time to find someone who would help her cut down the dead body of Mrs Perez from the beam. She had paid the men more than she could afford. Then, on her own, she had laid Ana's mother out on the table. She lit candles at her head and her feet. She folded Mrs Perez's arms on her chest and put the prayer beads in her hands. Finally, she covered Mrs Perez's white face with her black veil and placed her bible by her side.

Widow Silva felt bad leaving Mrs Perez alone – the custom was that the women of the town should sit in vigil – but these were not ordinary times. She had to think of the living. For hours, the rumbling of the Black Mountain had been getting louder.

When she was done, widow Silva left the Perez house for what she feared was the last time. Staying out of sight of the few soldiers still on patrol in the square, she headed for the town hall.

*

Ana and Carlos crept through the small wooden door and into the side chapel.

No one was there.

'It's all right, we're safe,' Ana said, adding the words 'for now' in her mind. Carlos had been so brave, but she could sense how scared he was.

Hand in hand, they ran up the nave and out into the alleyway. Ana peered around the corner, to see what was happening, just as widow Silva appeared in the far corner of the town square. Ana waved to attract her attention. Then, when she didn't appear to see them, Ana called her name.

'We're here!'

She and Carlos watched widow Silva looking for them in the semi-darkness – the moon was mostly covered by the cloud of ash – then raising her arm in reply. Ana pointed to the corner of the street that led down to the port.

A few moments later, they were together.

'Thank God, you're safe,' widow Silva said, putting her old hand on Ana's arm.

'Thanks to Carlos, I am.'

She felt her brother turn red. 'I didn't do much . . .'

'You showed great courage. Papa would have been proud of you.'

Ana looked around the empty square. Somehow, she had thought the town would be busy with people preparing to leave.

'Where is everyone?'

Ana watched widow Silva put her finger to her lips and point. Ana followed her gaze and, now, saw a pair of soldiers in the shadows near the town hall.

'The mayor imposed a curfew at dusk,' widow Silva explained. 'They are too scared to leave their houses.'

Ana was outraged. 'That's wicked! Anyone who stays is in danger.'

'Yes. But, sadly, Antonio didn't persuade many people that the danger was real. One or two have turned over their boats, and others have collected water from the pump just in case, but for most . . .'

Ana shook her head. 'Can't they see this is different? Don't they have eyes? Don't they have ears?'

The old woman sighed. 'There have been too many false alarms.'

'Even so . . .'

At her side, Ana felt Carlos pull at her sleeve. 'Do you think Pablo and Rudi are all right?'

Ana squeezed his hand. 'I'm sure they are,'

she said, with more confidence than she felt. She turned to widow Silva. 'Have you seen them?'

'Not for some hours.'

'We agreed to meet on the beach by the fishing racks,' Carlos said. 'Can we go there?'

Ana nodded. 'That's a good idea. You go down to the port. We will go back to the house to fetch—'

'No!' widow Silva cried, then covered her mouth with her hand.

Ana looked at her in surprise. Now she remembered Carlos had told her widow Silva was keeping her mother company. So why was she not still there?

'Mrs Silva?' From one look at the older woman's face, Ana could see something was seriously wrong. 'What is it?' Ana said. 'Please tell me.'

'Ana, I . . .'

Ana looked at her. 'We have to fetch my mother. Why don't you want me to go . . . ?'

But before widow Silva could answer, Ana felt Carlos jump.

'Look!' he said in a loud whisper. 'They are there! Over there.'

Ana followed his gaze and saw Antonio, Pablo and Rudi coming up the narrow street from the port. She only just managed to grab Carlos's arm before he shot out of their hiding place.

'The soldiers will see you.'

As the little group got closer, Ana could see that Antonio's face was bloody and bruised. Pablo was limping. Only Rudi, in his slow, stiff gait, was unharmed.

'What happened?' Carlos asked his twin when they drew level.

Pablo grinned. 'I twisted my ankle when I jumped over a wall getting away from the soldier. But I was quicker.'

Antonio gave a crooked smile. 'You should be very proud of these young men.' He looked at Rudi. 'All three of them.'

'I am.'

Ana looked at how one of his eyes was swollen shut and his hair was caked with blood. 'I have worked out what happened to my father, and why,' she said in a low voice.

'We will talk of it later, once we are safely away,' Antonio said. 'The boat is ready to sail.'

'*The* boat?' Ana said.

'He has a skiff,' Pablo spoke up. 'With two sets of oars.'

'And it has a mast and a sail,' Carlos added.

Ana raised her eyebrows.

'I have owned it for some time,' Antonio said. 'It is moored on the first jetty after the smoking racks.'

'I see.' Ana looked at her brothers, then smiled. 'It seems all the time you spend at the port has not been wasted after all.'

Pablo grinned. 'Antonio taught us how to keep the oars flat in the water.'

'In which case, go now with Antonio – you too, Rudi.' Ana turned to widow Silva. 'And we will fetch Mama, as much food as we can carry, and then meet you at the jetty.'

Chapter Eighteen

Without further warning, the ground began to shake violently. A crack appeared in the middle of the narrow street, like a mark of lightning.

'What's happening?' Carlos wailed, grabbing Ana's hand.

Ana heard a scream. She looked round the corner and saw people were opening their doors and coming out into the square.

She looked up to the Black Mountain looming over the town. There was another mighty rumble, as if the earth was groaning, then what sounded like an explosion underground. It was as loud as the cannons that were fired at the port to send an important ship on her way.

'We must hurry,' Antonio said.

'Should we find shelter?' widow Silva asked.

'No. We need to wait and see which way the lava will flow – it may run south rather than north towards the town – but the ash will still be deadly. I think we'll be safest on the sea.'

'My father said sometimes the sea rises up

and drowns the land,' Ana said. 'Might that happen?'

'It might,' Antonio said, 'but I think it will be the lesser of two evils.'

Ana paused, then nodded. They had to trust him. 'All right. We'll meet you at the boat as soon as we can.'

'We should ring the alarm,' Rudi said. 'To warn everyone that the mountain is erupting.'

'I'll come with you,' Pablo said. 'To help pull the bell.'

Ana saw the two boys, old enemies, reach an understanding.

Antonio put his hand on Carlos's shoulder. 'Carlos, come with me and help me load her up.'

They split up – Rudi and Pablo to the church, Antonio and Carlos to the port, leaving Ana and widow Silva.

'No one else is here,' Ana said. 'Tell me what's happened.'

Behind them, the grumbling underground was growing louder and louder.

'Ana, your mother's dead.'

For a moment, Ana felt as if she was frozen. Everything seemed to be happening in slow motion, as if she was under water. She caught her breath.

'I didn't want to tell you in front of the boys,' widow Silva said. 'I'm so sorry.'

Still, Ana said nothing. She didn't want to believe it. At the same time, she felt in her bones it was true.

In the church, the bell began to toll the alarm.

'I should go to her,' Ana said in a voice that didn't sound like it belonged to her.

'There's nothing you can do for her now,' widow Silva said.

Ana stared at her without seeing anything. 'What happened, do you know? Were you with her?'

Widow Silva shook her head. 'I found her. I have laid her out as she would have wanted.'

Ana snapped out of her trance. 'I must go to her.'

Widow Silva grabbed her arm. 'You must think of your brothers, you must think of yourself.'

Ana shook her head. 'I can't just leave her! It's not right! You can't think I would leave her—'

'Listen to me. They killed her, Ana. I saw her with my own eyes. I put her prayer beads in her hands and her bible beside her head. Nothing can harm her. We have to pray she is with your father now. But we must go. Don't you realise they will kill you if they find you? Pablo and

Carlos too.' Widow Silva looked up. 'If the mountain doesn't kill us first.'

Ana stood rooted to the spot, not sure what to do. There was a final mighty rumble, as if the whole world was breaking apart. Then, a noise such as she had never heard before; an explosion from deep inside the mountain. Moments later, a funnel of burning rock and fire shot up out of the crater, turning the night sky into red and orange and gold.

Suddenly, the town square was full of people. Ana saw the soldiers drop their weapons and run. Others fell to their knees and prayed, some were battening their doors with wooden boxes, as if they could possibly keep the river of fire out.

'Ana, we must go!' widow Silva cried.

All around them, in every direction, people were screaming and wailing. Liquid fire was erupting in every direction, like sparks from the blacksmith's anvil. Huge lumps of black rock were being hurled into the air and came crashing down on the slopes below.

There was yet another explosion. A flaming river of lava was starting to edge its way down towards the town. A cloud of hot ash was floating down over the town. No longer grey ash, but black.

'Black snow,' Ana said, remembering her father's warning.

Grief caught in her throat. Ana also knew that she would never forgive herself for leaving her mother unburied. The thought that she had died frightened and alone, a victim of brutal men, Ana knew would haunt her for the rest of her life. She knew widow Silva was right. To have a chance, they had to leave now.

'Ana?' the older woman said gently.

Ana vowed that, if they survived – if they all survived – she would bring the murderers of her father and mother to justice. She nodded. 'I understand. Thank you.'

As a third jet of molten lava and rock lit up the night sky, Pablo came racing out of the church with Rudi, who followed, as fast as his twisted leg would allow him, and rejoined Ana and widow Silva.

'Come on,' Ana said, before Pablo asked where their mother was. 'Mama is going to stay and pray for the town. She wants me to take you and Carlos to safety. She has faith God will save her.'

Pablo seemed to accept this. For all their lives, their mother had spent more time in church than anywhere else. She was less unhappy there.

Ana bit back her tears. She felt Rudi's eyes on her and she realised that he knew she wasn't telling the truth. To her relief, he said nothing. 'Hurry,' she said. 'We haven't got much time.'

Chapter Nineteen

'What do you mean?' demanded the mayor.

The priest looked to the door. 'What I say, brother. There are no soldiers. They have fled.'

The mayor and his brother were in the mayor's private rooms in the town hall.

'We should leave too. The horses are ready.'

The mayor was filling a wooden casket with treasure looted from the treasure ship *La Blanca*.

'Brother!' the priest said more sharply. 'We can't carry any more.'

The mayor looked at him. 'Shouldn't you be in the church with your flock? Praying for God to save us?'

The priest flushed. 'The carriage is waiting at the steps. We cannot delay. If the people see us going . . .'

'The "people",' said the mayor, with contempt, 'will not go against the soldiers.'

'I told you, the soldiers have gone.'

The room shook and a jagged crack appeared in the wall. Plaster fell from the ceiling.

'I beg you, brother,' the priest said, 'leave the rest. You have the most valuable things.'

The mayor snatched a few final items from the long wooden sideboard. It pained him to have to leave behind the gold bars and silver goblets. He thrust a handful of rubies and other jewels into his pockets.

'Here!' he shouted his orders. 'Come here!'

When no one came, he pointed to the priest to take one end of the casket and he took the other. Between them, they staggered out of the room and through the empty corridors of the town hall.

'Where are the guards?' the mayor demanded.

'It's what I've been trying to tell you. Everyone has gone.'

A flash of anger appeared in the mayor's eyes. 'I'll see them hung for deserting their posts.'

The two men – one in his priestly black, the other in his fine Spanish clothes – stumbled out onto the steps of the town hall. Below them, the square was a scene of disorder. Women and men were running in all directions as hot ash fell on their heads.

The mayor started to choke. He pulled a fine lace handkerchief from his pocket and held it over his mouth and nose. The carriage was waiting at the foot of the steps. The two horses were nervous, scraping the unsteady ground with their feet.

The groom sprang down and opened the carriage door. The mayor and his brother got in and stowed the casket at their feet. Then the groom climbed up to his seat, cracked his whip and the horses leapt forward towards the port.

The mayor stuck his head out of the window. 'Not that way, you fool! Take the coast road,' he shouted.

'But brother—' the priest tried to argue, but the mayor would not listen.

The driver swung the carriage around. With no care for anybody in its way – women, children or men – he followed his orders and headed for the old sea road going east.

Chapter Twenty

It was madness at the port. Ana had never seen anything like it. There seemed to be hundreds of people. Some were taking to the sea. Others were building places to shelter beneath the jetties or the fishing boats, hoping they would be protected against the ash and the lava.

'It's this way,' Pablo shouted.

Ana followed her brother. She felt numb. Her mother was dead, her father was dead. Perhaps not a single one of them would survive the night. The river of fire had split first into two, then into four. Now, it looked as if seven huge bands of lava were flowing out of the crater and towards the town. The cloud of black ash blotted out the moon and the sky. It was as if the world was ending.

'Here,' said widow Silva, handing Ana a basket.

Inside were smoked fish wrapped in a cloth, and a loaf of bread. Ana had dried fruit in her pocket and a goat's cheese she had managed to find as they ran down towards the port. It wasn't much. But so long as they had water to drink, they would be all right if they could keep away from the ash. Ana knew it would all depend on the direction of the wind.

They ran across the black sand towards the jetty. Ana held back, to make sure Rudi and widow Silva were keeping up.

Antonio and Carlos were waiting at the skiff. Ana was surprised. It was bigger than she'd expected. A long and low-bottomed rowing boat with a single mast and sail. Perhaps the rumours about Antonio being a Spanish nobleman were true.

Antonio held out his hand and helped widow Silva up the gang plank. Carlos hugged his twin, then looked around.

'Where's Mama?'

Ana opened her mouth, but it was Rudi who spoke. 'She is with other brave women in the church. They are praying for the town.'

Like Pablo, Carlos seemed to accept this. Ana was grateful. Somehow, Rudi had guessed something had happened to their mother.

'Thank you,' she whispered as he took the basket from widow Silva's hands.

'I'm sorry,' he whispered.

Ana felt a flood of affection for the outcast boy.

Then there was another jet of fire and rock from the crater.

'Quick,' Antonio said, pulling up the gang plank. 'We have to get as far away from the shore as possible.'

Ana looked around in despair. 'But how can we sail the ship without a crew?'

Antonio smiled, then winced at his swollen eye. 'Oh, we have a crew.'

Pablo saluted. 'Aye, aye, captain.'

'Carlos, can you cast off?' Antonio instructed.

Carlos ran to the stern of the boat and untied the mooring rope. Between them, they pushed the boat away from the jetty with the oars and then jumped into position.

Antonio was on the tiller to steer the skiff. Pablo and Carlos took an oar each and began to row. Slowly, they started to move away from the jetty. The port was full of small boats, all trying to make their way to the harbour mouth, but Antonio managed to steer them through the harbour mouth and out into the open sea.

'Raise the sail,' he shouted.

Pablo and Carlos rested their oars, then leapt up and hauled on the ropes to pull the mast up into place. Ana watched them with pride. She had no idea they were such good sailors and she wished her father could have known. Once the mast was up, Pablo released the rigging and the single, square white sail unfurled.

Fragments of rock were falling from the sky, raining down on the town and over the sea. Already, Ana could see their white sail was marked with grey ash. One boulder, larger than the others, landed in the water not far from the back of the boat. There was a smell of sulphur, as the rock sent up a jet of salt steam with a hiss.

But they caught a gust of wind and sailed further out into the choppy water. Ana only prayed that it would be far enough.

Flaming lumps of black rock, as large as a man's head, were thundering down the mountainside.

On the coast road heading east, the groom whipped the horses to go faster. On one side, there was the sheer wall of mountain. On the other, a drop down to the sea. Suddenly, he dragged on the reins to pull the horses up. Ahead, he could see the road was partly blocked. There must have been a landslide.

The carriage juddered to a halt.

The mayor put his head out of the window.

'Sir, we cannot get through!' the groom shouted. 'It's too dangerous.'

The mayor waved his hand. 'Nonsense. There's space enough for the carriage to pass.'

'The wheels of the carriage are too wide.'

The priest put his head out of the other window of the carriage. He looked worried.

'He's right. Brother, we should turn around.'

'Are you mad?' the mayor shouted. 'The lava flow is heading for the town. No, this is our best chance. If we can get to the other side of the headland, we'll be safe.'

The priest sat back in his seat.

'Get down,' the mayor shouted up to the groom. 'You can lead the horses through. The road is clear on the other side of the rocks.'

'Sir, with respect—' the groom began to say.

The mayor pulled a dagger from his belt. 'Do as you're told,' he said. 'Unless you want me to make the choice for you.'

Left with no choice, the groom jumped down from his seat. He hooked the reins over the horses' heads and tried to lead them through the rock slide. The carriage jolted, then jerked. The wheels began to turn. The groom could see how the eyes of the animals were wide with fear, but he talked to them in a low voice and they did what he commanded. He swung his broad riding coat over their heads to protect them from the falling ash.

Carefully, step by dangerous step, the carriage moved forward. They were almost through when the groom looked up and saw a huge black boulder hurtling out of the sky towards them. He shouted, and raised his arm. The horses reared up on their hind legs, their hooves flailing in the choking air. One of the hooves caught the groom on the side of his head and he fell, stunned, to the ground.

Terrified by the noise and the falling rocks, both horses reared up again. They were trying to get free of the wooden shafts joining them to the carriage. In their wild terror, the hooves of the first animal slipped in the ash, and it fell over the edge. Unable to keep its footing on the stones and rocks, it plunged down off the cliff edge, dragging the other horse and the carriage with it.

There was a strange pause, almost of silence. Then the groom, dazed, sat up. He saw at once how lucky he had been.

From the stern of the boat, Ana looked across the water back to the town.

The world was burning. Everything she knew had gone. The mountainside was aflame. And still jets of molten fire continued to shoot up out of the crater.

Ana swallowed hard. The slopes where they had played as children, their little white house above the vines, the goat she'd rescued from Antonio's, were in the direct line of one of the seven bands of fire. Their green pastures were being smothered by the lava. The land had turned black and the ash kept falling and falling. Choking the sky and the moon, the animals and the people.

Ana kept her eyes fixed on the Black Mountain and wondered if anything would survive. If they would survive.

Her father's words were ringing in her head – the seven maidens in the sky, like the seven islands. On that night in January, five months ago, he had said they were lucky.

'But what would you say now, Papa?' Ana said, fighting back her tears.

Saturday, 15 May 1706

Ten days later

Chapter Twenty-One

In Antonio's skiff, they sailed away in the early hours of Wednesday, 5 May – the day when the eruption began. With Pablo and Carlos as his crew, Rudi and Ana helping, Antonio caught a trade wind and steered them around the headland to safety.

They came ashore the following day and, after a few hours' climbing up from the coast, found an abandoned shepherd's hut to the west of the Black Mountain. The lava had flowed north and east, leaving the land to the west almost untouched. The sky was dark. There was no day and no night. But they were alive, they were safe.

In the distance, they could see the fire still coming from the heart of the volcano. They could still hear the cracking of the earth. But the lava flow was nowhere near and the wind was blowing the choking black ash in the opposite direction. There was fresh water. The abandoned hut seemed as good a place as any to take shelter and see what happened.

They had been waiting for ten days.

At dawn, on Saturday 15 May, Ana stepped outside the humble building they had made their home. Antonio had risen early and gone out, and widow Silva was still sleeping. Straight away, she felt that something was different. She took a deep breath, then realised. On this Saturday morning, the sky was blue. The air was clear. The sun was shining. She could see for miles and miles and miles.

The Black Mountain had fallen silent.

For a moment, Ana simply stared around her. She had never seen anything so beautiful. She almost didn't dare believe it. Then, joy and relief flooded through her and she shouted over her shoulder.

'Wake up! Pablo, Carlos, Rudi – wake up!'

Inside the hut, three sleepy boys raised their heads from the straw mattress on the floor, blinking at the new day. Widow Silva, dozing in an armchair beside the empty fireplace, stirred from her rest. She stood stiffly and came outside too.

'What is it?' she asked. 'Is something wrong?'

'I think it's over,' Ana said. 'It's over.'

Then the words caught in her throat as she realised what it meant. She took widow Silva's hand to stop herself from falling. Antonio had told her that sometimes volcanoes erupted for years. She had thought they might never be able to go home. This had been only ten days. In the end, they had been lucky after all. Just as her father had promised.

'It's over,' she said again to herself.

Now Pablo and Carlos came tumbling out of the hut, followed by Rudi.

'Look around us,' Ana said, waving her arms wide to take in the view. For more than a week, they had lived in a place of twilight and dread. Now, suddenly, there was a new world at their feet.

For a while, the little group stood in silence. There was both everything – and nothing – to say. Then, Ana had the need to explore more and see for herself.

'Shall we climb to the headland and see if we can find Antonio?'

The boys' eyes sparkled with excitement.

'I'll stay here and get the fire going,' widow Silva said. Ana saw there were tears in her eyes.

*

They set off.

Ana could see the island looked different. There was jagged black rock where once there had been green fields. There were pillars of lava and black dunes where once there had been trees. Here and there, she saw a dragon tree still standing or a copse of cedar trees.

As they climbed higher, Ana began to see some parcels of land had also been spared. The lava flow had divided, carving a direct route north down from the mountain to the sea. Black ash had covered the land to the east. But on their side of the mountain, a few vines had survived in parcels of land.

'There's Antonio,' cried Carlos, pointing ahead.

Ana saw Antonio standing on the ridge. He must have woken even earlier than she had and gone to see if anything could be saved. Ana began to hope there might be something.

He smiled as she and the boys drew level.

'It's all gone,' Carlos said, looking at his twin. 'The port, all the ships, all gone.'

Together, they stood looking down over what once had been the most important harbour on Tenerife. The sea wall had been swept away and there were several tiny black islands of lava in the bay. Most of the town had been buried beneath the river of fire and ash. Ana caught her breath, imagining the fear and despair of those who left it too late to flee.

'Not quite all,' Antonio said. 'Look again.'

Here and there, a few white buildings in the town were glittering bright. They were scorched and some were almost rubble, but they were still standing. The harbour master's house had not been swept away. Ana could just make out a few upturned fishing boats on the beach.

'I think I can see the spire of the church,' said Rudi.

'And I can see the roof of the town hall,' said Pablo.

Carlos looked up at his sister. 'Does that mean we can go home and find Mama?'

Ana knew Antonio was looking at her. She had told him everything. How her father had discovered that the mayor himself had planned the sinking of *La Blanca*. How she believed the mayor's men had stolen the treasure, while pretending to be a rescue mission. Then, how they had scuttled the ship with the loss of all on board and her father had seen it happen from the clearing on the mountainside.

Ana also told Antonio how she thought her

mother had told the priest what her husband had seen when she went to confession at church. The priest, in turn, had told his brother the mayor. That had signed Mrs Perez's death warrant too.

Ana had intended to tell the boys their mother was dead when the time was right. Once she was sure the danger from the volcano was over. That time had come sooner than she had expected, but Ana knew she had no choice.

'Come and sit with me, Carlos,' she said, patting the grass beside her. 'You too, Pablo.'

The twins exchanged a nervous glance. Rudi went to stand with Antonio.

'Our father was a brave man,' Ana began. 'He always stood up for what he believed. He had courage and that is why—' She took a deep breath. 'That is why he was killed.'

'Killed?' Pablo said. Carlos looked at the ground.

Ana waited, but neither of them asked more. She understood. They wanted to hear – but also could not bear to hear. The twins were still young. When they were older, she would tell them everything. Not yet.

'As you know, our mother found life hard,' she said carefully. 'But she, too, had great courage.

116

She knew what was right. She died protecting her husband's memory. She died to protect us.'

Beside her, Carlos began quietly to cry. Ana put her arm around him and felt Pablo lean against her shoulder.

Far below, in the valley, the church bell of the old town began to ring out across the blackened land.

Sunday, 15 May 1707

One year later

Chapter Twenty-Two

As the summer of 1706 turned to autumn, and autumn turned to winter, other families came back.

Like Ana, they wanted to rebuild their lives. They wanted to rebuild the town they loved. There was no sign that this little fishing village had ever been the major port of Tenerife. The water was too shallow and the rocks of black lava in the sea made the sailing treacherous. The ships still came from Spain, but now they docked in the bustling harbour on the north-east coast of the island. In time, that new port would become the capital city. Their little village on the island's north-west coast was forgotten by all except those who lived there.

When the crimes of the mayor and his brother came to light, the new council of the town made Ana and her family an apology. The groom who had tried to drive the mayor and his brother to safety told them everything. The carriage was found at the foot of the cliff with the two dead horses still attached to the shafts. The bodies of the mayor and the priest were inside. The casket of treasure had split open, scattering rubies and precious stones all around. Some of that wealth had been spent on rebuilding the town hall.

The town council had cleared Ana's father's name and her mother's death was recorded as murder. Though their bodies had been lost in the eruption, a white headstone in the churchyard read: 'Tomas Perez and Maria Perez, who died in the service of the town they loved.'

Ana visited each week with her brothers to lay flowers on the grave.

On Sunday, 15 May 1707, a church service was held to remember all those who had died. Everyone was wearing their best clothes and hats.

It was a year to the day since the eruption had finished. Many people had died, choked by the ash or buried alive in their homes as the lava flowed down the mountain and buried part of the town.

Ana bowed her head. She prayed for her father and her mother, but also for all those others who had lost their lives one year ago. Antonio and widow Silva, her brothers Pablo and Carlos, and their closest friend, Rudi, were beside her in the pew.

Rudi was fifteen now. As he had grown taller, his spine had become less bent. His twisted arm was stronger from building houses and pens for animals, and from helping farmers plant new vines and fruit trees. He would never be as agile as Pablo or Carlos, but he was a broad and fine young man.

Ana lifted her eyes to the stained-glass windows of the church and let the voices of the choir wash over her. The music lifted her spirits. The sun sent glinting patterns of coloured light over the altar. The council members had offered Ana a patch of land to the west of the town to make up for what her father had lost. She was to own it as a woman in her own right. When the service was over, Ana was due to present herself at the town hall to sign the papers.

Ana didn't know what she was going to do.

She fixed her gaze on the black robes of the new priest, a young man from another of the Canary Islands. He was eager and kind and Ana thought he was an excellent addition to their tiny community.

'In the name of the Father, the Son and the

Holy Spirit,' the priest said. He raised his right hand in the air and made the sign of the cross.

'Amen.'

Everyone answered, some loudly and others, like Ana, to themselves under their breath.

'Amen.'

The service was over.

The priest was standing at the door to greet each member of the congregation in turn. He smiled at Ana and the boys, he gave a small bow to widow Silva and shook Antonio's hand.

Outside in the town square, the sun was shining. Ana stood for a moment just taking in the scene. The town hall itself was still standing, though the walls were cracked. There was wooden scaffolding set up in the private gardens so that the damage to the roof could be mended. The white stone steps, where Antonio had tried to persuade the townspeople to listen, were broken. There were ridges of lava where the flow had come into the heart of the town. It made the surface uneven.

Away from the square, in the area mostly untouched by the eruption, new houses were being built. Tradesmen were opening shops – selling cloth and books and earthenware pots, anything that people might need. Most families had lost everything, but their little white town was coming back to life. It would never be the same, but it was a good place to live all the same.

Ana knew she belonged here. But as for her brothers? She wasn't sure.

She lifted her hand to shield her eyes against the bright sunlight as Antonio came to stand beside her.

'Have you decided?' he asked.

'It depends what Rudi says.'

'You know what he will say,' Antonio said. 'Do you want me to come with you to the town hall?'

Ana shook her head. 'It's something I should do on my own. If I go.' She turned to look at him. 'Does your offer still stand?'

'Of course. Pablo and Carlos both have a natural talent for the sea. You saw that. Any captain would be glad to have them. When they are old enough, I will buy them both a commission.'

'Thank you.'

Ana bit her lip. Her brothers seemed so young, but they were nearly thirteen years old. In a year's time they would be old enough to enlist and join the crew of a ship. Ana was overcome with emotion. They would sail away from the island. She might never see them again.

'Speak to Rudi,' Antonio said gently.

Not trusting herself to speak, Ana nodded.

'Come to the house when you are finished,' he said.

Antonio now owned a fine house with wooden balconies overlooking the water. He had told Ana his life story. He was the only son of a rich merchant from the south of the island. After an argument, Antonio had left the family home and never returned. On the death of his father, he had become a wealthy man. He inherited his father's estate, which he sold, and he bought a house and land in northern Tenerife instead. Antonio no longer needed to hide himself away on the mountain. Instead, he took his place as one of the leaders rebuilding the town.

'Have courage,' Antonio said, patting her shoulder. Then he turned to find the boys, who were leaning against the wall by the church.

'Pablo and Carlos, are you hungry?'

'I could eat a horse,' Pablo said.

'How would you like to join me for lunch? Mrs Silva has been kind enough to say she will come.'

'What about Rudi and Ana?' Carlos asked.

Pablo jabbed him in the ribs with his elbow. As usual, Carlos looked at his boots.

'Rudi and Ana will join us as soon as they can,'

Antonio said. 'Come. Let's go and see what my housekeeper has prepared for us.'

As Ana watched her little family walk away towards the beach, she knew she was delaying. She was nervous about the conversation to come.

'Is something the matter?' asked Rudi.

'Will you walk with me for a moment?' Ana said.

'If you wish,' Rudi said.

They fell into an easy pace. Rudi still had a limp, but it was less obvious. Up and down the tiny streets they strolled, their bodies casting shadows on the ground as they went in and out of the sun.

The church bell began to chime for twelve o'clock. Ana glanced up at the clock. The town council was expecting her. She couldn't keep them waiting. She couldn't delay any longer.

She took a deep breath. 'Rudi, I hope you know I think of you as another brother.'

At her side, she felt him turn red. 'I had always hoped you did.'

'We have all been through so much together.'

'Yes.'

Ana chose her words carefully. 'Pablo and Carlos are good boys . . .'

Rudi nodded. 'The best.'

'However, they do not love the land as I love the land. Or as you love the land.'

Rudi grinned. 'No. They prefer the sea.'

'They always have.' Ana laughed. 'My father could never understand it, though he accepted it. They had no interest in growing vines. It's why he taught me everything he knew.'

'You know as much as any man,' Rudi said loyally. 'More.'

Ana paused. This was the moment. She didn't want to put Rudi on the spot. At the same time, if he did not want to accept her offer it was better to know. Better to know sooner rather than later.

'The town council has offered me a new patch of land to grow vines,' she said, looking over to the town hall. 'They are expecting me to sign the papers today. I would own the land absolutely and in my own right.'

'I had heard that,' Rudi said carefully.

Ana turned to look at him. 'The thing is, Rudi, I cannot possibly do it on my own. I will need a foreman, someone to help plant the vines, oversee the workers, harvest the grapes.'

'Yes?'

Now Ana thought she heard a trace of hope

in his voice. It gave her the courage to keep going.

'What I want to know is if you would be that person, Rudi. You must feel free to say no. The last thing I want is for you to feel that you owe me something.' Ana was aware she was talking too fast and too much. 'I cannot think of anyone I would rather have helping to rebuild my father's business. Widow Silva will continue to live with us and run the house. You can either remain living at Antonio's house, or, if you prefer, you could come and live in the house with me and the boys, and there would be—'

Ana felt the rest of her words crushed out of her as Rudi threw his arms around her and gave her a hug, before stepping back.

'Yes!' he shouted. 'I can't believe that you would think my answer would be anything but yes.'

'Oh—' Ana gave a sigh of relief. 'Oh, I'm so glad.'

Then Rudi tilted his head to one side. 'What do Pablo and Carlos think? Do they agree with this plan?'

Ana nodded. 'Yes. I talked it over with them first, and then with Antonio and widow Silva. Everyone thinks it's a wonderful idea.'

A huge smile broke across Rudi's face. He gave a deep bow. 'In which case, Miss Perez, I am honoured to accept your offer.'

Ana slipped her arm through Rudi's and together they retraced their steps to the town hall. Today is the beginning of the next adventure, Ana thought. For all that had happened, for all of the loss she had endured, that the town had suffered, she felt a new hope for what the future might bring.

Over the sea, the gulls followed the fishing fleet. In the window boxes of the town, the first of the summer flowers were a brilliant pink and red and yellow. And high above them to the south, proud against a blue sky, the Black Mountain was quiet.

For now.

Acknowledgements

I'd like to thank everyone involved in helping this short novel reach the page, in particular the legendary Fanny Blake, the brilliant Maria Rejt and everyone at Pan Macmillan, including Alice Gray, Samantha Fletcher, Marian Reid and Liz Cowen. A big thanks, too, to my agent Mark Lucas at The Soho Agency, together with Niamh O'Grady and Alice Saunders, everyone at The Reading Agency, and all the teachers, librarians, booksellers and support staff who make sure each book in the Quick Reads programme finds its readers.

About Quick Reads

"Reading is such an important building block for success"
- Jojo Moyes

Quick Reads are short books written by best-selling authors. They are perfect for regular readers and those who are still to discover the pleasure of reading.

Did you enjoy this Quick Read?
Tell us what you thought by filling in our short survey. Scan the QR code to go directly to the survey or visit https://bit.ly/QuickReads2022

Turn over to find your next Quick Read...

A special thank you to Jojo Moyes for her generous donation and support of Quick Reads and to **Here Design**.

Quick Reads is part of The Reading Agency, a national charity tackling life's big challenges through the proven power of reading.

www.readingagency.org.uk
@readingagency   #QuickReads

The Reading Agency Ltd. Registered number: 3904882 (England & Wales)
Registered charity number: 1085443 (England & Wales)
Registered Office: 24 Bedford Row, London, WC1R 4EH
The Reading Agency is supported using public funding by Arts Council England.

Supported using public funding by
**ARTS COUNCIL
ENGLAND**

Find your next Quick Read: the 2022 series

Available to buy in paperback or ebook and to borrow from your local library.

More from Quick Reads

Continue your reading journey

The Reading Agency is here to help keep you
and your family reading:

Challenge yourself to complete six reads
by taking part in **Reading Ahead**
at your local library, college or workplace
readingahead.org.uk

Join **Reading Groups for Everyone** to find a
reading group and discover new books
readinggroups.org.uk

Celebrate reading on **World Book Night**
every year on 23 April
worldbooknight.org

Read with your family as part of the
Summer Reading Challenge
at your local library
summerreadingchallenge.org.uk

For more information, please visit our website:
readingagency.org.uk

If you liked *The Black Mountain*, why not try
the first book in Kate Mosse's latest series

The Burning Chambers

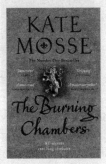

Carcassonne 1562. Nineteen-year-old Minou Joubert
receives an anonymous letter at her father's bookshop.
Sealed with a distinctive family crest, it contains just five
words: *SHE KNOWS THAT YOU LIVE.*

But before Minou can decipher the mysterious
message, a chance encounter with a young Huguenot
convert, Piet Reydon, changes her destiny forever. For
Piet has a dangerous mission of his own, and he will
need Minou's help if he is to get out of La Cité alive . . .

A thrilling adventure, and a heartbreaking love story,
Europe awaits in *The Burning Chambers*. A historical novel
of excitement, conspiracy and danger like no other . . .

*

'A powerful storyteller with an abundant imagination'
Daily Telegraph

'An irresistible read' *Prima*

Out now

Discover the second instalment in
Kate Mosse's bestselling new series

The City of Tears

May 1572. For ten violent years the Wars of Religion have raged across France. But now a precarious peace is in the balance: a royal wedding has been negotiated, an alliance between the Catholic Crown and Henri, the Huguenot King of Navarre. It is a marriage that could see France reunited at last.

Meanwhile, an invitation has arrived for Minou Joubert and her family to attend this historic wedding in Paris in August. But what Minou does not know is that the Joubert family's oldest enemy, Vidal, will also be there. Nor that, within days of the marriage, her family will be scattered to the four winds and one of her beloved children will have disappeared without trace . . .

The City of Tears is a story of one family's fight to stay together, to survive and to find each other, against the devastating tides of history . . .

*

'[A] dramatic, immersive tale of secrets, conspiracies, fanaticism and loss' *Daily Mail*

'Magnificent, epic' Marian Keyes, bestselling author of *Grown Ups*

Out now